little bea

daniel roode

GREENWILLOW BOOKS
An Imprint of HarperCollinsPublishers

Adobe Illustrator and Adobe Photoshop were used to prepare the full-color art.

The text type is 24-point Martin Gothic URW T Light.

Library of Congress Cataloging-in-Publication Data

Roode, Daniel.

Little Bea / by Daniel Roode.

p. cm.

"Greenwillow Books."

Summary: From morning to night, Little Bea buzzes through her neighborhood helping friends and having fun.

ISBN 978-0-06-199392-3 (trade bdg.)   [1. Bees—Fiction.]

I. Title.   PZ7.R6713Li 2011   [E]—dc22   2009053681

11 12 13 14 15 LEO 10 9 8 7 6 5 4 3 2 1

First Edition

 Greenwillow Books

For Mom and Dad, and Laura

Up, up, up comes the sun.

A little bee spreads her wings and yawns.
"Good morning, Little Bea," says the sun.
"It's time to start the day!"

Bzzz. Bzzz. Bzzz!

Little Bea scoots from her flower and takes off.

Flutter. Flutter. Flutter. Hello, Butterfly!

Bzzz. Bzzz. Bzzz.

Little Bea buzzes as she flies by.

Knock, knock!

"Whooooooo's there?" says Owl.

"It's Bea."

"Bea who?"

"Be my friend and come play with me!"

Hoo-hoo-hooray!

Duck.

Duck.

Beaver is gathering pears, and Little Bea helps.
"Come back for pie tomorrow," says Beaver.
Bzzz. Bzzz. Bzzz. Yum!

Tug. Tug. Tuuuuug!
Little Bea helps Rabbit in his garden.
"One, two, carrots for you!"
Munch, munch, crunch.
"Thank you for lunch, Little Bea."

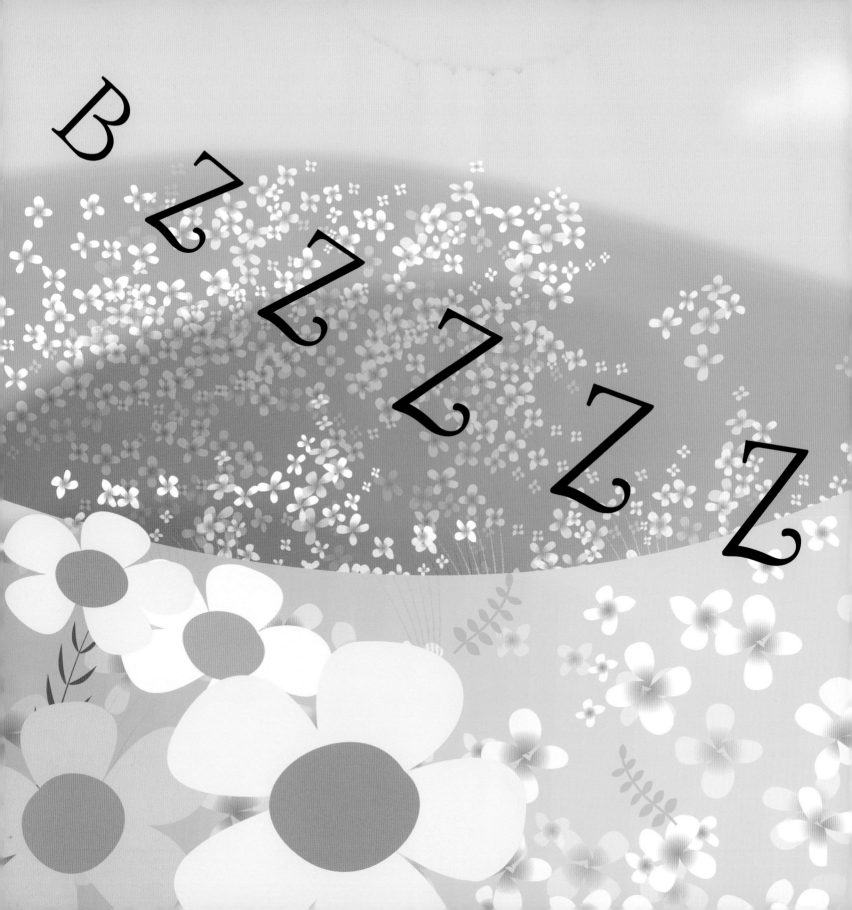

"Grrreetings, Little Bea," says Bear.
A flower for Bea.
Honey for Bear.
Bea and Bear love to share.

"Peekaboo! I see you!"

"I see you, too," says Deer.

Pitter. Patter. Drip. Drip. Drop.
Rain. Rain. Rain.
"I love the rain!" says Mouse.
"Let's play!" says Little Bea.
Bzzz! Bzzz! Splash!

"Chirp, chirp, chirp," says Cricket.
"Look, Little Bea, the sun is setting."

Bzzz. Bzzz. Bzzz.
Time to go home.

"Follow me!"
says Firefly.
Blink. Blink. Blink.

Up, up, up comes the moon.
Little Bea's friends are sleeping.
It's time for Little Bea to go to sleep, too.

"Hushhh . . . ," says the moon.

Good night, Little Bea.
Bzz. Bzz. Zzzzzzzzzzzzzz.